Once Upon ANOTHER TIME

by **CHARLES GHIGNA** and
MATT FORREST ESENWINE

illustrated by **ANDRÉS F. LANDAZÁBAL**

beaming books
MINNEAPOLIS

for Charlotte and Christopher —C.G.
for Jennifer, my Natural Gal —M.F.E.

27 26 25 24 23 22 21   1 2 3 4 5 6 7 8 9

Hardcover ISBN: 978-1-5064-6054-3
Ebook ISBN: 978-1-5064-6657-6

Library of Congress Cataloging-in-Publication Data

Names: Ghigna, Charles, author. | Esenwine, Matt Forrest, author. |
    Landazábal, Andrés, illustrator.
Title: Once upon another time / by Charles Ghigna and Matt Forrest Esenwine
    ; illustrated by Andrés F. Landazábal.
Description: Minneapolis, MN : Beaming Books, 2021. | Audience: Ages 3-8. |
    Summary: Illustrations and easy-to-read, rhyming text introduce the
    reader to the world as it was before humans made their mark, then
    propose going outdoors--without electronic devices--to connect with that
    ancient beauty.
Identifiers: LCCN 2019056908 (print) | LCCN 2019056909 (ebook) | ISBN
    9781506460543 (hardcover) | ISBN 9781506466576 (ebook)
Subjects: CYAC: Stories in rhyme. | Nature--Fiction. | Natural
    history--Fiction.
Classification: LCC PZ8.3.G345 Onc 2021 (print) | LCC PZ8.3.G345 (ebook)
    | DDC [E]--dc23
LC record available at https://lccn.loc.gov/2019056908
LC ebook record available at https://lccn.loc.gov/2019056909

VN0004589; 9781506460543; DEC2020

Beaming Books

510 Marquette Avenue

Minneapolis, MN 55402

Beamingbooks.com

Once upon another time
in a land of long ago,
mountains peeked up through the clouds,
bright with fallen snow.

Rivers rushed through canyon walls.
Rainbows rose from waterfalls.

Wonder waited in the hush
of every new sunrise.
Flocks of sparrows rode the breeze
and filled the morning skies.

The land was fresh, the air was clean,
the valleys lush with shades of green.

There were no cities made of steel,
no buildings, no concrete,
no highways, byways,
billboard signs,
no traffic in the street.

There were no drones or airplanes
flying past a smoggy sun.
There were no phones or internet—
the webs were spider-spun!

Before our tools and grand machines,

before we harnessed wind and streams,

before we mined for gold and oil,
before we learned to work the soil,

before one human step was taken . . .

Earth and moon
and stars awakened.

Once upon another time,
the world was young and new.

If you want to know this world,
there's something you can do . . .

Leave behind the phones and screens,
and take a step outdoors.

Breathe in air that once was shared

Feel the wind
upon your skin.
Imagine where
that wind has been.

Hold an oak leaf. Trace its veins.

Chase a rainbow. Taste the rain.

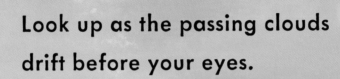

Look up as the passing clouds
drift before your eyes.

Behold, their wondrous dance unfolds—
a ballet in the skies.

Walk through sunny fields of grass.

Climb a maple tree.

Smell the clover, wild and sweet.

Listen to the bees.

Pitch a tent.
Watch the moon.
Listen to
the crickets' tune.

And to the sky the sun will climb . . .

. . . just as it did another time.